# THE FORT IN THE DARK NIGHT

**HARSHIT**

This book is dedicated to my mother Mrs. Kavita Rao and my father Mr. Surendra Kumar.

# Contents

# Acknowledgements

My mother helped helped me in typing the book . Also my english teacher Ankit Sharma sir helped me in grammatical mistakes .

# Preface

In this book there are some spine chilling ghost stories . I have tried my best and as everyone of us likes ghost stories weather they believe in ghost or not . This book is best for ghost story lovers , the stories in this book are all fictional which consistes some paranormal activities.All the stories are different from each other and there is no connecetion between them.

## Does ghosts really exist ?

No one knows weather ghosts exist or not this is on you if belive in them or not, but first law of thermodynamics proposed by albert einstein says energy cannot be created or destroyed but only changes form and as we know that the soul inside the human body is a type of energy.

# Contents

# 1
## The Fort

———❤———

*In the city of Ajmer rumors were spreading that the fort outside the city was haunted and there was treasure in it's first chamber . In that same city two friends named Parag and Nitish lived , both of them were very good friends and don't belive in ghosts at all . So they both decided to go to that fort and get that treasure . After some days Parag got a message from Nitish that they are going to get that treasure tonight . So , Parag got ready and packed all instruments and also packed some empty sacs for filling that treasure . After some time the moon came up and again Parag got a message from Nitish that they both will meet at that first chamber so , Parag lifted all the things that he had paked and drived to that fort . After reaching there he opned his phone to call Nitish but there were already some messages from nitish and they were like .*

*1. You are not doing good.*

*2. You are going to die.*

*3. This is your last day on the earth.*

So , Parag dialed to Nitish for asking him that what he wanted to say , but there was someone laughing strangely on the another side . Then Parag called there anoher friend Mayank who then told him that some days before Nitish

# 2
# Cricket

Once upon a time there a boy named Kunal , he loved to play cricket . Everyone told him that , he should join an acadmy but , he was not so rich to join an acadmy . One fine day while he was playing cricket in a local ground , a man came to him and told him that he played very good cricketand he should join an acadmy . So , Kunal replied him that he was so poor to join an acadmy or buy an cricket kit . Then that man told him to come in the morning at 3:30 A.M. if he want to learn cricket professionally . Then during the whole night Kunal thought about it and then decided to go at morning . In the morning Kunal wake up at 3 o'clock and then went to that ground and after reaching there he searched for that men for around 30 minutes and then turned back to return to his home thinking that , that men has prancked him and he is not going to come but after turning he saw that , that man was standing just in front of him with an expensive kit bag , a pair of sports shoes and some of the accessories . There that man told him that his name is Yashraj Singh and he was a former coach . After some months , one day while practicing Kunal hit a shot straight to his coach's mouth but to his surprise , that ball passed through coach's head . Suddenly coach's mouth and eyes turned white and he started screaming at Kunal . At that time Kunal was so much scared that he took his kit and ran away to his home . After some years Kunal was selected Rajasthan's state cricket team for playing Ranji Trophy due to his tallent and hardwork . One day while he was talking to his team mates he told his story to his team mates then one of the seniour player of them told him that once upon a time Yashraj Singh was coach of our team but one day while he was bowling a boy hit a shot which directly hit coach's mouth and he died on the spot .

# 3

## College Trip

Once upon a time there was a college group consists of 15 boys and 10 girls decided to go to a picnic . There are 3 friends who were packing some things for the trip , then suddenly a boy came and challenged them to puncture the bus tire in between the trip , so those friends excepted the challenge . After some time the trip started in a very nice way . A few hours later at the time of sunset those 3 boys rememberd about that challenge and a soon afte they punctured all the bus tires when the bus was stopped for a small break . But by mistake they punctured the bus in the middle of the junjle . So after some time they decided to call on emergency helplines but there was no signal . So then they decided to stay in the tents which were brought by them for camping . Then the same boy again came to them and challenged them three he told them that there was an old house nearby and they all have to stay there for an hour . Then they all 3 accepted the challenge and decided to go there at night . After some time the moon was up in the sky so they came out of there tents with some torchs and cameras . A few minutes later they were in the middle of the hall of the house , in the first ten minutes everything was normal but after that some strange and horrefied voices started comming and they seems like someone is crying or laughing creepily . A few seconds later , a voice of breaking of something came from back side so , they turned backward . One of them shouted 'oh my god' , because there was a woman in white cloths full of blood , shouting . So them all started all around one of them jumped out of an window in hurry and ran until they reach there tents . when they wake up the rescue team was there , then they were rescued and those 3 boys were taken to the hospital because there legs were broken due to jumping from height .There they were asked that how their legs were broken so , they told there whole story to teachers , doctors and the rescue team but after some search it was found that there was not any such house and there was also not any such boy .

# 4

# Brijraj Bhawan Palace

Once upon a time there were two friends named Ravi and Rohit both of them were students of arts and were given an assignment to visit any five historical places and write everything about them . So , both of them decided to go to Brijraj Bhawan Palace ,Kota . They both packed there bags and rented a car to go there due to some of delays they reached Kota at night . Instead of sleeping they decided to explore and write about that place as they were already late and if they will not submit there assignment at time they will not get marks . So , they started exploring and writing about that place , then suddenly a helper came who have covered his mouth with a mask and he was dressed like a royal britishman and was also speaking english so much fluently that they felt a little bit strange . After some time when Ravi have just finished the assignment and turned back to show the assignment to Rohit but he was not there and even that helper was missing . So , he started seaching for Rohit . Aftre some time he reached near a room from where some strange voices were comming . So he got inside that room there he so that someone was sitting on a table and was writting something nearby he saw that his friend's dead body was lying . So in hurry he turned back to run but the door was locked and due to the sound caused that man turned his face totally updown towards Ravi he was that same englishman helper . He looked verymuch scary , he also have some signs of bullets on his face , suddenly he threw a knife which then directly stricked Ravi's mouth and he died on the spot .

# 5

## The Shortcut Route

Once upon a time there was an auto driver named Tilak , usually he returns to his home till 10'o clock at night but today it was already 11:30 and still he was in the city because today there was an function in the city . So, while he was going to his home he decided to take the shortcut route which passes though the junjle . So Tilak was driving on his highest speed as he was already late . Sounds of animals were regularly coming from the jungle . Suddenly he saw towards the jungle there he notices that there were two red lights coming , he ignores them as he was too much scared and wants to go to his home as fast as he can . After every few minutes those red lights and sounds of animals are coming from the jungle . A few seconds later from somewhere there came a traffic policeman in between the path and signaled Tilak to stop his auto but as the speed of the auto was very high Tilak was unable to control it and accidently his auto crashed into that officer , a few seconds later auto stopped and Tilak came out from the auto searching for the body but it was not there so , he paniked and got inside the auto suddenly his side got on the front mirror of the auto there he saw that , that policeman was sitting just behind him on the backseat of the auto so Tilak tried to escape from there but that policeman was holding Tilak's neck . When Tilak saw in the mirror clearly he saw that policeman's face was fully white and his neck was torn . Somehow he escaped from that auto and ran towards the forest there he thought that , that red light was coming from the city so he followed that light , when he reached near that light he saw that a woman was sitting on a tree her face was full of blood so , Tilak once again started running soon , he reached city and got into the police station which was just in front of him there and senior inspector told him that once upon a time a boy and a girl full drunken were going on a bike , and when a traffic inspector stopped them the boy killed him and no one knows that what happen to that girl .

# 6

## The Store Room

It is the story of my 7th class . At that time in my class a rumor was rising that the store room of our school was haunted . Once on the republic day my friend Nilesh and I were walking in the building of my school because the function was delayed due to rain and bad weather . We were talking about that haunted store room and mocking it as we don't belive in any such things suddenly , we were infront of that store room it was locked then I said something to my friend but not reply came so , I turned backward but Nilesh was no there and when I looked again towards that store room its door was open so , I decided to go inside . I thought that Nilesh have also got inside that store room so , I looked for him everywhere in the store room but he was not there suddenly I saw that Nilesh was sitting in a cornor with a baseball bat in his hands , he was growling there . So , I called his name a few times . suddenly , he turned his face backward , his face was full of blood and it was regularly bleeding from his head . He started coming towards me with that bat . Some how I escaped from him but I faint after coming out from that room . When I woke up I saw I was fully surrounded by the teachers . Teachers told me that I was severely injured and was bleeding from my head and I have been fainted for 5 days . Then I told my story to the teachers . then teachers replied me that a few days before a boy hit Nilesh with a baseball bat . And a few days after Nilesh died due to severe injury .

# 7

# My Neighbour

Once upon a time when me and my family were going from hotel to home on a christmas night while my sister requested my parents to by her a toy . So , my father stop the car near a toy store . My father told me to stop in the car until they come . So I decided to here to music till they come . While I was listening to songs and enjoying them suddenly sounds of screaming of some one came on my ear phone and then all the lights in the car started flickering then I saw that a strange man with a iron stick . Soon he started striking our car . So , for protecting my self I hid under the seat and after few time I realised that my parents have came so I rose up and to my surprise that man was not there and even all the broken glasses of the car were alright so , I thought that my mind have played a trick on me . After some time we reached our home and I was so much tired that I directly got inside my bedroom and startrd listing to songs , after some time that sounds of screaming again started and lights started flickering . And when my sight got on the window I saw that , that same man with iron stick smiling strangely was there breaking windows of my room so , I closed my eyes and started screaming . When my parents came into my room I opened my eyes and surprisingly no windows were broken , also no such men was there and even no lights were flickering , Then I told my story to my parents . Then after asking some peoples we came to know that once upon a time in our neighbour once there lived a mad man who was died in an accident .

# 8
## Women In The Red Cloths

It was a fine sunny day with a great weather . And today Rishab is going to deliver his speech on republic day . So , he left home early while he was walking he felt that someone was following him so , he gave a sight backward there he saw that a dreedful looking woman in red clothes was also walking just behind him but somehow he managed to ignore her . After some time Rishab's turn come to deliver his speech , during his whole speech he saw that , that same woman in red cloths was impatiently all around the ground . After the speech got over he get out of the stage and searched all around the ground for that lady but he was unable to find her . After the function got over . He started walking to his home . But after walking approx halfway someone pushed him so much hardly that he fall in between the road but somehow he managed to overcome the injury and started running . After a few days while he was walking on the terrace with his father after walking for a while he saw that , that woman was on the terrace nearby suddenly Rishab felt headache , his body suddenly stopped working and he fell unconcisious . Afer a few days of comma his eyes open in the city hospital there he telled everything what happened to him to his mother . But his mother was preparing him for his school but suddenly his mother noticed that there was a red bracelet in Rishab's hand then his mother asked Rishab that where did he found it , hen Rishab answerd that he found that bracelet on the pathway . Then his mother pulled out that bracelet and then broked it down . After that time Rishab have never seen that woman .

# 9
# The House On The Road

Once when I was coming from my office to my home at 2 o'clock at night . My house was initially 6 km. away from my house everything was going right until my new brought bike broked down then I decided to walk until I find any vehicle or any house or hotel to stay for the night as it was a dark night and it was only jungle all around for kilometers . After walking for half an hour I found an old house . I entered inside it , it was totally ruined and there were animals and insects all around , in my bag I have some food , some files and a laptop . After entering I ate the food and then sleapt . A few hours later I woke up because I heared a few sounds I first thought that it was any animal teasing me by making sounds but after noticing the sound for some time I get to know that the soun was like breaking of glass or breaking of a plate or breaking of any tumbler made up of china clay , so I decided to explore this house , after a few seconds I have seen a thing like a shadow or some thing like a strange creature it was laughing strangly and growlig creepely so I ran away but that creature also started following me after some time I fall due to a rock at that time I first saw that creature's face it looks dreedful somehow I managed to ran away from there after running for a few minutes I found my name written on the road with the help of blood after watching it my head starting rolling and I fainted after that I don't know what happen to me next . Next day I was founded fainted in a graveyard by auto driver . After this incident I changed my office and I have never again dared to go from that road and even I can't even step outside from my house .

# 10
## The Bet

Once upon a time there were three friends named Ravi , Rahul and Irfan . One day while they all are talking with each other Irfan challenged Ravi that if he stay in any graveyard for one hour at 12o'clock of night Irfan will give him three thousand rupees so Ravi excepts the challenge . Then Ravi decides to go their todays night he did all the preprations like he packed torches , cameras and many other things . At night Ravi reached the graveyard after some time he sendes a video to both Irfan and Rahul in which he was touching things related to some graves and laughing on them . After some time Rahul messages Ravi to not to touch those things related those graves and also said not to mock at them but Ravi replies that there are no things like ghostes these are just superstetions . For some days everything got well but one day Ravi got a gift box but after opening it he gets horrified because there were some things which Ravi have touched , that day his furniture started moving by itself the door gets knocked by itself but after he opens there was no one outside . Deprresed from all these things one day he sucided . But before dying he messaged his friends that his body is being controled by someone . This case is still an mystry for police but still police says that Ravi's menatl health was not good so he commited sucide . But his friends says that , that ghost of grave was teasing Ravi because he mocked on him and thats why that ghost get upset and have taken it's revenge from Ravi . And till the date this case is an mystry .

" It's never easy to lose but life is not all sunshine and rise " - AB de villiers @jersy number 17

AB DE VILLIERS

Congratulating Indian mens cricket team for winning international mens t20 world cup 2024 - 25 .

Team India

As I personally love cricket so my idles are AB DE VILLIRES and K.L. RAHUL .

K.L. Rahul

IDLE

## AB DE Villires

26